W9-AGP-679

THE SPIDERWICK CHRONICLES™

BEWARE THE BOGGART!

Jared Grace's Guide to Defense Against FANTASTICAL CREATURES

by Irene Kilpatrick
based on the screenplay by
Karey Kirkpatrick and David Berenbaum, and John Sayles
from the books by
Tony DiTerlizzi and Holly Black

Simon Spotlight
New York London Toronto Sydney

SIMON SPOTLIGHT

An imprint of Simon & Schuster Children's Publishing Division

1230 Avenue of the Americas, New York, New York 10020

™ & © 2008 Paramount Pictures. All Rights Reserved.

Photograph of dandelion on page 23, copyright © Paul Mutton

Manufactured in the United States of America

First Edition

2 4 6 8 10 9 7 5 3 1

ISBN-13: 978-1-4169-4946-6

ISBN-10: 1-4169-4946-1

Contents

A Fantastical World

My name is Jared Grace. Not too long ago I moved with my sister, Mallory, and my twin brother, Simon, to Spiderwick Mansion. The mansion was a strange old house; its kitchen was stocked with tons of weird things, like tomato sauce and honey. On our first night there we found a family portrait of our great-aunt, Lucinda Spiderwick, as a girl. She had lived in the mansion until a few years ago, when she went to a nursing home.

ME!

I discovered a hidden study upstairs that once belonged to Aunt Lucinda's father, Arthur. And I came across a book he wrote about what he called the "fantastical world." At first I thought it was something he made up—until I came face-to-face with a brownie, a hobgoblin, a griffin, some sprites, a pack of goblins, and a very dangerous ogre!

In the following pages I will tell you about what I've been through and show you how to protect you and your family from dangerous creatures. Beware: This stuff could happen to anyone! The invisible world reaches right up to your doorstep— and maybe even *inside* your home.

SIMON

AUNT LUCINDA

MALLORY

The Sight

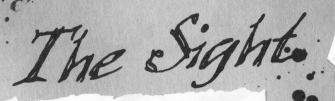

The most important tool you need is the Sight. Without it you won't be able to see creatures like goblins, brownies, and trolls—unless they choose to show themselves. Here's how you can get the Sight:

Are you the seventh son of a seventh son? The seventh daughter of a seventh daughter? Are you a redhead? If you can say "Yes!" to any of these questions, then you may be in luck!

Many people like you are **born** with the Sight.
Find a seeing stone—a stone with a natural hole in its center—and look through it. Better yet, make a contraption like the one we found in Arthur Spiderwick's study!

Get a hobgoblin like Hogsqueal to owe you a favor or give him a bird to snack on. Then politely ask him to spit in your eye.

GROSS!!!!!

Rub faerie ointment on your eyelids. You can also use faerie bathwater—but it is kind of gross and isn't as effective. Faerie ointment is made from four-leaf clovers.

Look through any kind of circle. It won't work as well as any of the things I've mentioned, but it's better than nothing!

Key ring

ring

doughnut (with a hole)

rubber band

The Guardian of the Home

The first skirmish in our household—not counting the fights I've had with Simon and Mallory—was with Thimbletack, our brownie. If we had known about brownies when we moved in, I don't think we would have had so many problems! First of all, we destroyed his nest in the wall. Then I read the Field Guide even though he warned me not to. Thimbletack was just trying to follow Arthur Spiderwick's instructions to protect the guide and keep it in the mansion. All in all we did a great job of making Thimbletack *really* angry.

How to detect a brownie:

Small objects disappear. Example: Mallory's fencing medal

You hear noises like skittering footsteps inside walls or along the floor. For a while we thought we had a squirrel living in the mansion! Brownies are invisible when they want to be, and they can fit into very small spaces. This makes it easy for them to sneak up and surprise you.

You find a "nest." Aha! That's where all the lost stuff went! Typical brownie nests can include objects such as cloth, lace, leather, dolls, dollhouse furniture, matchbooks, lead soldiers, and all sorts of shiny things, like keys, medals, and coins.

You see writing in the dust appear before your eyes. If the words rhyme, you definitely have a brownie!

You find your pets out of their cage—and you're sure you locked it!
Example: Simon's mice

You see tiny brownie tracks around the house.

Tip:
Sprinkle sugar or flour on surfaces the brownie might cross. Footprints will show up better. It's a good idea to ask a grown-up if this is okay first. Otherwise you might have more than just brownie troubles!

Look Out for Boggarts!

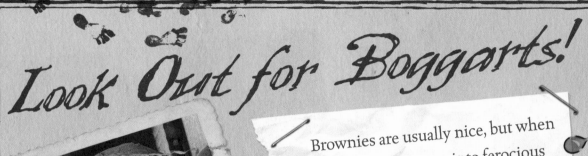

Brownies are usually nice, but when they get mad, they turn into ferocious boggarts! Boggarts are mischief makers. They will do anything to annoy the people in your house, and they like to make you look guilty.

Signs that you have a boggart in your house:

You upset a brownie.

Note: Boggart tracks are almost identical to brownie tracks, but they look kind of **mean**.

You see tiny boggart tracks around the house.

Common pranks:

Common pranks:

1.) Tying your hair to the bed
2.) Cutting your eyelashes
3.) Filling your shoes with mud or another gross and squishy substance
4.) Tying your shoelaces together
5.) Someone makes a huge mess of the house (kitchens are popular targets for boggart tantrums)—and it wasn't you

My eyelashes!

YIKES!

NOT ME! Yuck!

"The boggart did it!"

If a boggart is on a rampage, remember that you don't have to fight *everything*. You can calm seemingly harmful creatures, like boggarts, and some may even help you against worse enemies.

To turn a boggart back into a harmless brownie:

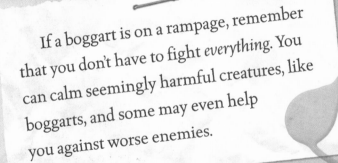

A boggart would like a new nest if you've destroyed the old one. A birdhouse, like the one we gave Thimbletack, is just the right size.

It's also a good idea to apologize. Just say it loudly where you think the boggart might be, or write him a note.

Remember that boggarts like honey.

Tip. Memorize this useful phrase: "The boggart did it!"

Defense Tips

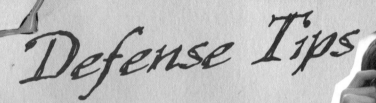

After we were able to get Thimbletack to calm down, we had to learn how to protect ourselves against scarier creatures outside the mansion. Even though I defended Spiderwick Mansion, I know you can use these tactics in any kind of home: From an apartment in the city to an igloo in the Arctic, the rules are the same.

1. If there's a charmed circle of protection around your home, great! Just make sure bad creatures don't figure out how to break the circle. And if they do, stay inside until the moon rises. That should buy you some time.

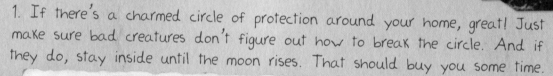

2. Make sure everyone who needs protection is with you. Goblins could take someone hostage and try to bargain with you, but you can't trust them! Also, the more people on your side, the better.

I had Mallory, Simon, Mom, Thimbletack, and Hogsqueal (if you can count him) with me against a whole horde of goblins plus one ten-foot ogre (Mulgarath).

3. If creatures get through the circle of protection, or if you don't have one, guard each possible entrance with a sealing or protection charm (see page 19). Don't forget the chimney! If someone really wants to come in, they'll look *everywhere!* You can also pour extra salt along door thresholds as an added protection.

4. Wear red. Don't wear green! Red will protect you from faeries, but green will attract them to you. Only wear green when you're around friendly faeries!

5. Protect yourself from yourself. Ogres can tell if you're lying just by looking at you. So the less you know, the better. Don't let them know what you know. As a girl, Aunt Lucinda escaped Mulgarath this way. So did Simon.

A Recipe for Fantastical Success

Most of these items can be found at any grocery store. And one piece of advice: You may want to ask your parents for permission before you try any of these!

Oatmeal glued on with rubber cement! :)

In case you get hungry: peanut butter, jelly, bread

Shopping list o' supplies

* Honey—boggarts like honey a lot!
* Oatmeal—a faerie protection
* Tomato sauce, juice, or any kind of tomatoes, fresh or canned—burns goblin skin like acid
* Salt—blinds goblins

We used a bicycle pump filled with salt!

Vinegar—the fumes make goblins choke

vinegar in a spray bottle

J.G.

Goblin bombs (Simon's recipe)
Combine in largest vessel possible
(a bathtub works well):
30 jars of tomato sauce, 15 boxes of oatmeal,
20 boxes of salt. Stir ingredients together.
Pour into small plastic bags and seal tightly.
You can also pour some into spray bottles.
(Don't forget to ask a grown-up for permission first!)

Charms

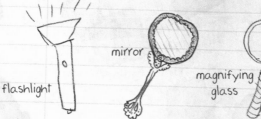

Sealing charm—will also burn goblins on contact
Black pepper, bay, rosemary, salt, red ribbon,
pouch (such as a sock, scarf, or glove).
Combine the herbs and spices in the
pouch, then tie it with the red ribbon.
Bind the pouches across window latches
and other locations near entries into the house.

Protection charm—Aunt Lucinda used this one!
One twig of oak tree, one twig of ash
tree, one twig of thorn tree. Bind all three
twigs together with red thread. Hang from
bedposts or near entrances.

flashlight

mirror

magnifying
glass

Useful objects for
seeing different creatures,
especially at night.

Any salt
will do.
You can
use these.

In case they get you, always keep a first-aid kit handy!
Stop any bleeding with a clean cloth, rinse the wound with water,
apply an antibiotic cream, and cover the wound with a bandage.
If a grown-up can help you with this, even better!

Weapons

Antique saber →

Real weapons can work well against the enemy, but you should be careful not to hurt yourself or other humans! Mallory was already taking fencing lessons, so she had a foil (and some pretty handy skills!), and we found a saber in the mansion.

Mom with a Kitchen knife!

↑ Steel cuts and burns

Meat cleaver

Baseball bat—can come in handy.

Other useful items:

*Kitchen knives

*door locks

*armoires

*pans

*forks

*picks

The Enemy

Always think carefully about what kinds of creatures you're dealing with! Goblins, ogres, trolls, griffins, and sylph each have their own strengths and weaknesses.

Goblins — How to tell if goblins are nearby:

1.) Small pets go missing. (This means the goblins have grabbed Fluffy for food.)

2.) You have more nightmares than usual.

3.) There's a hole in the garbage can. Goblins like to scavenge—they will eat your trash, and they might take sharp objects like pieces of glass or thorns to use as teeth.

Other tips:
* Don't confuse hobgoblins with goblins. Hobgoblins like to make trouble but don't mean any harm. Goblins are just plain *mean*.
* Goblins have a terrific sense of smell. Once they have the scent, they can track creatures that are underground!

Ogres

One weakness of ogres that you can use to your advantage: They love to hear the sound of their own voices. If you can get one to start bragging, that can be a handy distraction.

You can tell an ogre by its large (and pointy) horns and fangs. Ogres like Mulgarath can shape-shift into creatures of any size, but only for a short time. Mulgarath often chose to transform into a crow. Don't let your eyes deceive you; if someone you know appears out of the blue, make sure you know who they **really** are before you let them into your house!

Trolls

Keep an eye out for trolls. They're pretty hard to miss: They're big and scaly. There are many different kinds of trolls. Mallory and I were scared out of our wits by a mole troll once. Mole trolls can make huge underground tunnels, and they're very speedy underground even though they have poor eyesight. I've found that the best way to get a troll off your back is to have a truck slam into it.

How to summon Byron
(in the Tree Elf language):
Grip, Grap, Greep
Niffgri Eras Eralc Seke
Ehcop Sirhc Yert-Yerak
Imas, Aiam, Nnifl

This noble creature looks like a cross between a lion and an eagle.
Make sure to treat it with respect! Griffins don't usually go near
people, but some—like Byron—can become loyal to humans.

Sylph

No images of sylph exist, but they look something like this.

Sylph are tiny winged creatures
that fly in swarms. From far
away they can look like cotton or
dandelion seeds. Sylph like to sing,
but don't listen to them! Their song
will mess up your concept of time.
This is how Arthur Spiderwick was
lost for eighty years. He had no
idea how long he was gone.

Remedy: Bring ear plugs or
some music to block out the
hum of the sylph!

Now that I've told you just about everything I know, I hope you've found it all useful. I'm sure there are many more things to learn about dealing with dangerous creatures, but I hope that you never have to learn them. Just in case, though, keep this book handy. And good luck!

If you discover anything new, be sure to draw it here—and add a description!